First
SONGS &
ACTION RHYMES

Jenny Wood

Illustrated by Chris McEwan

Aladdin Books
Macmillan Publishing Company
New York

Maxwell Macmillan International Publishing Group
New York   Oxford   Singapore   Sydney

THIS BOOK BELONGS TO

First Aladdin Books edition 1991
First published in 1990 by Conran Octopus Limited,
37 Shelton Street, London WC2H 9HN

Text copyright © 1990 by Conran Octopus Limited
Illustrations copyright © 1990 by Chris McEwan

Aladdin Books
Macmillan Publishing Company
866 Third Avenue
New York, NY 10022

Collier Macmillan Canada, Inc.
1200 Eglington Avenue East
Suite 200
Don Mills, Ontario M3C 3N1

Printed in Italy
1 2 3 4 5 6 7 8 9 10

Library of Congress CIP data is available

The illustrations in this book suggest, for appropriate rhymes,
the actions that may accompany them. You and your child
may like to follow these or to improvise your own.
☆ indicates those songs for which music is given at the end of the book.

CONTENTS

LULLABIES

Hush, hush, little baby,
  The sun's in the west;
The lamb in the meadow
  Has lain down to rest.
The bough rocks the bird now,
  The flower rocks the bee,
The wave rocks the lily,
  The wind rocks the tree.
And I rock the baby
  So softly to sleep,
She must not awaken
  Till daisy-buds peep.

The Man in the Moon looked out of the moon,
   Looked out of the moon and said:
"'Tis time for all children on the earth
   To think about going to bed!"

Hush-a-bye, don't you cry,
   Go to sleepy, little baby.

When you wake, you shall have cake
   And all the pretty little horses.

Blacks and bays, dapples and grays,
   Coach and six white horses.

Golden slumbers kiss your eyes,
Smiles await you, when you rise.
Sleep, pretty darling, do not cry,
And I will sing a lullaby.

The evening is coming, the sun sinks to rest,
The birds are all flying straight home to their nests,
"Caw, caw," says the crow as he flies overhead,
It's time little children were going to bed.

Here comes the pony, his work is all done,
Down through the meadow he takes a good run,
Up go his heels—and down goes his head.
It's time little children were going to bed.

The sandman comes, the sandman comes,
 He brings such pretty snow-white sand,
For every child throughout the land,
 The sandman comes.

Bye low, bye low,
 Baby's in the cradle sleeping;
Tiptoe, tiptoe,
 Still as pussy slyly creeping;
Bye low, bye low,
 Rock the cradle, baby's waking;
Hush, my baby, oh!

Rock-a-bye baby, so sweet and so fair
   While mother sits by in her old rocking chair,
With her foot on the rocker the cradle she swings,
   And though baby slumbers he hears what she sings.

Rock-a-bye baby on the treetop,
   When the wind blows, the cradle will rock,
When the bough breaks, the cradle will fall,
   And down will come baby, cradle and all.

Rock-a-bye, rock-a-bye, nothing to fear
   Rock-a-bye, rock-a-bye, mother is near;
With her foot on the rocker the cradle she swings,
   And though baby slumbers he hears what she sings.

Sleep, baby, sleep,
   Thy father guards the sheep,
Thy mother shakes the dreamland tree,
   And from it fall sweet dreams for the
Sleep, baby, sleep.

Hush, little baby, don't say a word!
  Papa's going to buy you a mocking bird.

And if that mocking bird don't sing,
  Papa's going to buy you a diamond ring.

And if that diamond ring turns to brass,
  Papa's going to buy you a looking glass.

And if that looking glass gets broke,
  Papa's going to buy you a billy goat.

And if that billy goat won't pull,
  Papa's going to buy you a cart and bull.

And if that cart and bull turn over,
  Papa's going to buy you a dog called Rover.

And if that dog called Rover don't bark,
  Papa's going to buy you a horse and cart.

And if that horse and cart fall down,
  You'll still be the sweetest little baby in town.

Baby's boat's a silver moon
  Sailing in the sky,
Sailing o'er a sea of sleep
  While the stars float by.

Sail, baby, sail
  Out upon that sea;
Only don't forget to sail
  Back again to me.

Baby's fishing for a dream,
  Fishing far and near,
Her line a silver moonbeam is,
  Her bait a silver star.

Sail, baby, sail,
  Out upon that sea;
Only don't forget to sail
  Back again to me.

Sleep, my baby, sleep now and rest,
    Safe as a fledgling in its wee nest.
Sleep now and rest, safe in your nest.
    Sleep, my baby, sleep.

Lullaby, and good night,
    In the sky stars are bright,
Round your head, flowers gay
    Scent your slumbers till day.
Close your eyes now and rest,
    May these hours be blest.

FIRST SONGS

This is the way the ladies ride:
    Nimble-nim, nimble-nim.
This is the way the gentlemen ride:
    Gallop-a-trot! Gallop-a-trot!
This is the way the farmers ride:
    Jiggety-jog, jiggety-jog.
This is the way the butcher's boy rides:
    Tripperty-trot, tripperty-trot,
Till he falls in a ditch with a flipperty,
    Flipperty, flop, flop, FLOP!

Dance, little baby,
　Dance up high,
Never mind, baby,
　Mother is nigh.
Crow and caper,
　Caper and crow,
There little baby,
　There you go!
Up to the ceiling,
　Down to the ground,
Backward and forward,
　Round and round.
Dance, little baby,
　Dance up high,
Never mind, baby,
　Mother is nigh.

Jelly on the plate,
　Jelly on the plate,
Wibble wobble,
　Wibble wobble,
Jelly on the plate.

Two little eyes to look around,
Two little ears to hear each sound;
One little nose to smell what's sweet,
One little mouth that likes to eat.

Little girl, little girl, where have you been?
Gathering roses to give to the queen.
Little girl, little girl, what gave she you?
She gave me a diamond as big as my shoe.

Bobby Shaftoe's gone to sea,
    Silver buckles on his knee;
He'll come back and marry me,
    Bonny Bobby Shaftoe!

Bobby Shaftoe's young and fair,
    Combing down his yellow hair;
He's my love for evermore,
    Bonny Bobby Shaftoe!

To market, to market,
  To buy a fat pig;
Home again, home again,
  Jiggety-jig.

To market, to market,
  To buy a fat hog;
Home again, home again,
  Jiggety-jog.

To market, to market,
  To buy a plum bun;
Home again, home again,
  Market is done.

Ride a cockhorse to Banbury Cross,
  To see a fine lady upon a white horse;
Rings on her fingers,
  And bells on her toes,
She shall have music wherever she goes.

Trot, trot, trot,
  Go and never stop.
Trudge along, my little pony,
  Where 'tis rough and where 'tis stony.
Go and never stop,
  Trot, trot, trot, trot, trot!

A trot, a canter,
  A gallop and over,
Out of the saddle
  And roll in the clover.

Father and Mother and Uncle John
  Went to market, one by one,
Father fell off!
  Mother fell off!
But Uncle John went on, and on,
  And on, and on, and on.

This little cow eats grass,
  This little cow eats hay,
This little cow looks over the hedge,
  This little cow runs away.
And this BIG cow does nothing at all
  But lie in the fields all day!
We'll chase her
  And chase her
    And chase her!

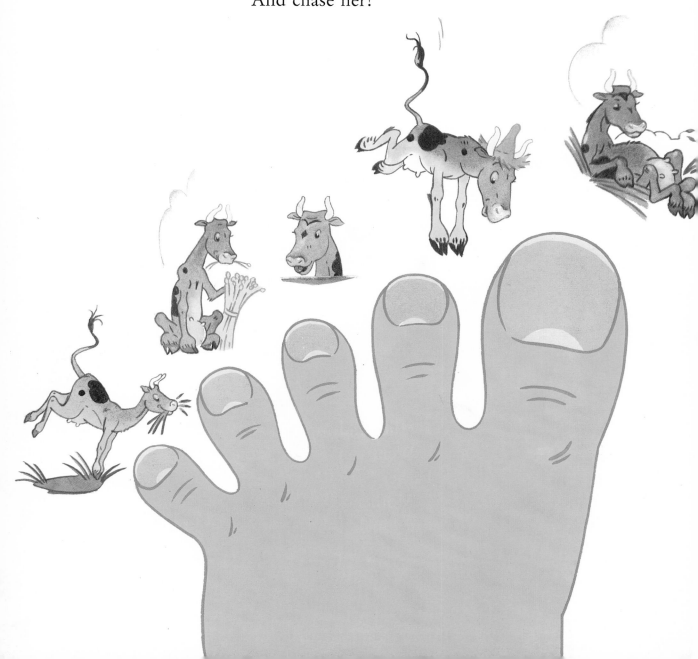

This little pig went to market,
　This little pig stayed at home;
This little pig had roast beef,
　This little pig had none.
And this little pig cried:
　"Wee-wee-wee-wee-wee,"
All the way home!

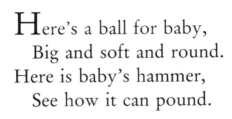

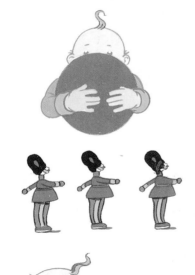

Here's a ball for baby,
    Big and soft and round.
Here is baby's hammer,
    See how it can pound.

Here are baby's soldiers,
    Standing in a row.
Here is baby's music,
    Clapping, clapping so.

Here is baby's trumpet,
    Tootle-tootle-oo.
Here's the way the baby
    Plays at peek-a-boo.

Here's a big umbrella,
    To keep the baby dry.
Here is baby's cradle,
    Rock-a-baby-bye.

Peek-a-boo, peek-a-boo,
Who's that hiding there?
Peek-a-boo, peek-a-boo,
Baby's behind the chair!

Where, O where, has my little dog gone?
　O where, O where, can he be?

With his tail cut short, and his ears cut long,
　O where, O where, has he gone?

Clap, clap hands, one, two, three,
　Put your hands upon your knees,
Lift them high to touch the sky,
　Clap, clap hands and away they fly.

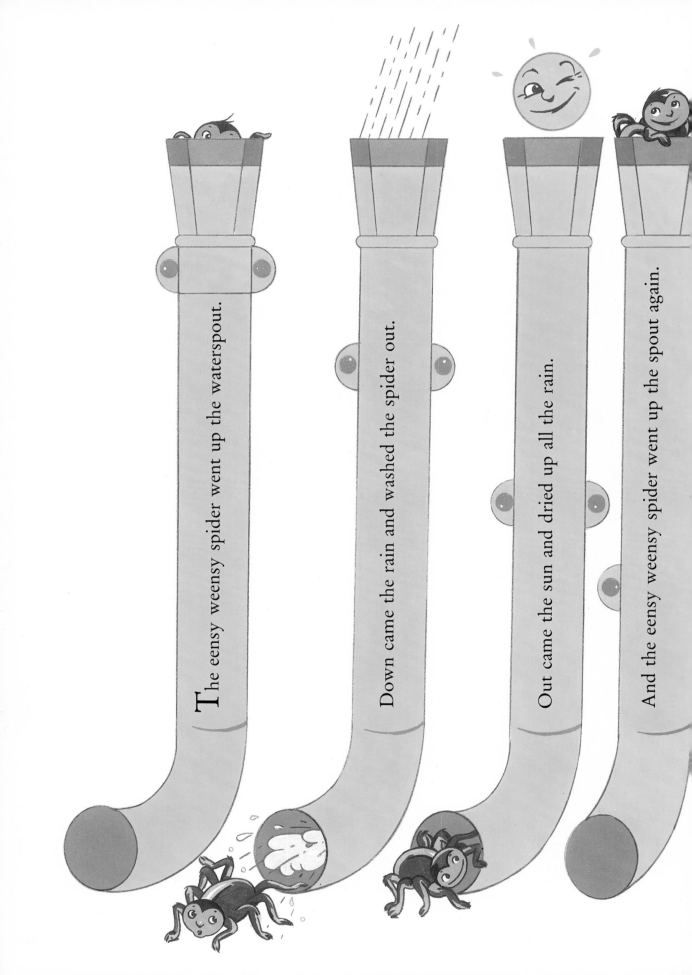

The eensy weensy spider went up the waterspout.

Down came the rain and washed the spider out.

Out came the sun and dried up all the rain.

And the eensy weensy spider went up the spout again.

Little Arabella Miller
   Found a hairy caterpillar.
First it crawled upon her mother,
   Then it crawled upon her brother.
All said: "Arabella Miller,
   Take away that caterpillar!"

Slowly, slowly, very slowly
   Creeps the garden snail.
Slowly, slowly, very slowly
   Up the wooden rail.

Quickly, quickly, very quickly,
   Runs the little mouse.
Quickly, quickly, very quickly,
   Round about the house.

Hickory, dickory, dock,
  The mouse ran up the clock.
The clock struck ONE.
  The mouse ran down,
Hickory, dickory, dock.

An elephant goes like this and that.
   He's terrible big,
And he's terrible fat.
   He has no fingers,
And he has no toes,
   But goodness gracious, what a nose!

Row, row, row, your boat,
   Gently down the stream.
Merrily, merrily, merrily, merrily,
   Life is but a dream.

ACTION RHYMES

Jack-in-the-box jumps up like this.

He makes me laugh when he waggles his head.

But Jack-in-the-box jumps up instead.

I gently press him down again.

Five little monkeys
   Jumping on a bed.
One fell off
   And bumped his head.
Mama phoned the doctor
   And the doctor said:
"No more monkeys
   Jumping on a bed."

Four little monkeys . . .

Three little monkeys . . .

Two little monkeys . . .

One little monkey . . .

I'm a little teapot, short and stout.
　Here is my handle,
Here is my spout.
　When I hear the teacups, hear me shout,
"Just tip me over, pour me out."

Clap your hands, clap your hands,
　Clap them just like me.

Touch your shoulders, touch your shoulders,
　Touch them just like me.

Tap your knees, tap your knees,
　Tap them just like me.

Shake your head, shake your head,
　Shake it just like me.

Clap your hands, clap your hands,
　Then let them quiet be.

We are soldiers marching along,
  Left right, left right,
Singing a song;
  Hands by side,
Heads quite still,
  Down the street and up the hill.

29

I have ten little fingers
    And they all belong to me.
I can make them do things,
    Would you like to see?
I can shut them up tight,
    Or open them all wide;
Put them all together,
    Or make them all hide.
I can make them jump high;
    I can make them jump low;
I can fold them quietly,
    And hold them all just so.

Here is the sea, the wavy sea,
  Here is the boat and here is me.
And the little fishes down below
  Wriggle their tails, and away they all go.

I hear thunder, I hear thunder,
  Hark, don't you? Hark, don't you?
Pitter-patter raindrops,
  Pitter-patter raindrops,
I'm wet through–
SO ARE YOU!

Moppety-mop and Poppety-pop
   Went on their way with a skip and a hop
One with a skip and one with a hop,
   Moppety-mop and Poppety-pop.

Stepping over stepping-stones,
   One, two, three,
Stepping over stepping-stones,
   Come with me.
The river's fast,
   And the river's very wide,
And we'll step across on stepping-stones
   To reach the other side.

Can you hop like a rabbit?
  Can you jump like a frog?
Can you walk like a duck?
  Can you run like a dog?
Can you fly like a bird?
  Can you swim like a fish?
And be still like a good child—
  As still as this?

Teddy bear, teddy bear, dance on your toes.

Teddy bear, teddy bear, touch your nose.

Teddy bear, teddy bear, stand on your head.

Teddy bear, teddy bear, go to bed.

Teddy bear, teddy bear, wake up now.

Teddy bear, teddy bear, make your bow.

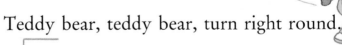

Teddy bear, teddy bear, touch the ground.

Teddy bear, teddy bear, turn right round.

Teddy bear, teddy bear, run upstairs.

Teddy bear, teddy bear, say your prayers.

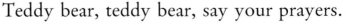

Teddy bear, teddy bear, turn off the light.

Teddy bear, teddy bear, say good night.

With my little broom I sweep, sweep, sweep;
On my little toes I creep, creep, creep.
With my little eyes I peep, peep, peep;
On my little bed I sleep, sleep, sleep.

Mix a pancake, stir a pancake,
Pop it in the pan.
Fry a pancake, toss a pancake,
Catch it if you can.

Bears, bears, everywhere!
Climbing stairs
Sitting on chairs
Collecting fares
Painting squares
Bears, bears, everywhere!

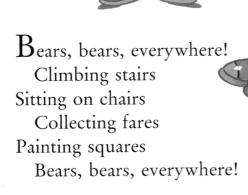

Oh, we can play on the big bass drum,
    And this is the way we do it:
BOOM, BOOM, BOOM goes the big bass drum,
    And that's the way we do it.

Oh, we can play on the little flute,
    And this is the way we do it:
TOOTLE, TOOTLE, TOOTLE goes the little flute,
    And that's the way we do it.

Oh, we can play on the tambourine,
    And this is the way we do it:
TING, TING, TING goes the tambourine,
    And that's the way we do it.

Oh, we can play on the . . .

FIDDLE, DIDDLE, DEE goes the violin . . .

TICKA, TICKA, TECK go the castanets . . .

ZOOM, ZOOM, ZOOM goes the double bass . . .

TA, TA, TARA goes the bugle horn . . .

Handy Pandy, Jack-a-dandy,
    Loves plum cake and sugar candy,
He bought some at the grocer's shop,
    And out he came, hop, hop, hop!

Down at the station, early in the morning,
    See the little puffer bellies all in a row.
See the engine driver pull the little handle.
    Chug! Chug! Whoo! Whoo! Off we go.

If you're happy and you know it,
  Clap your hands.
If you're happy and you know it,
  Clap your hands.
If you're happy and you know it,
  And you really want to show it,
If you're happy and you know it,
  Clap your hands.

If you're happy and you know it,
  Nod your head . . .

If you're happy and you know it,
  Say "Ha! Ha!!" . . .

If you're happy and you know it,
  Do all three . . .

Can you walk on tiptoe,
　As softly as a cat?
And can you stamp along the road,
　Stamp, stamp, just like that?

Can you take some great big strides
　Like a giant can?
Or walk along so slowly,
　Like a poor, bent old man?

The farmer's in the dell,
  The farmer's in the dell,
High-ho the derry-o,
  The farmer's in the dell.

The farmer picks a wife . . .

The wife picks a child . . .

The child picks a nurse . . .

The nurse picks a dog . . .

We all pat the dog . . .

One finger, one thumb, keep moving,
One finger, one thumb, keep moving,
One finger, one thumb, keep moving,
We'll all be merry and bright.

One finger, one thumb, one arm, keep moving . . .

One finger, one thumb, one arm, one leg, keep moving . . .

One finger, one thumb, one arm, one leg, one nod of the head, keep moving . . .

LEARNING RHYMES

One, two,
    Buckle my shoe;

Three, four,
    Knock at the door;

Five, six,
    Pick up sticks;

Seven, eight,
    Lay them straight;

Nine, ten,
    A big fat hen;

Eleven, twelve,
    Dig and delve;

Thirteen, fourteen,
    Maids a-courting;

Fifteen, sixteen,
    Maids in the kitchen;

Seventeen, eighteen,
    Maids in waiting;

Nineteen, twenty,
    My plate's empty.

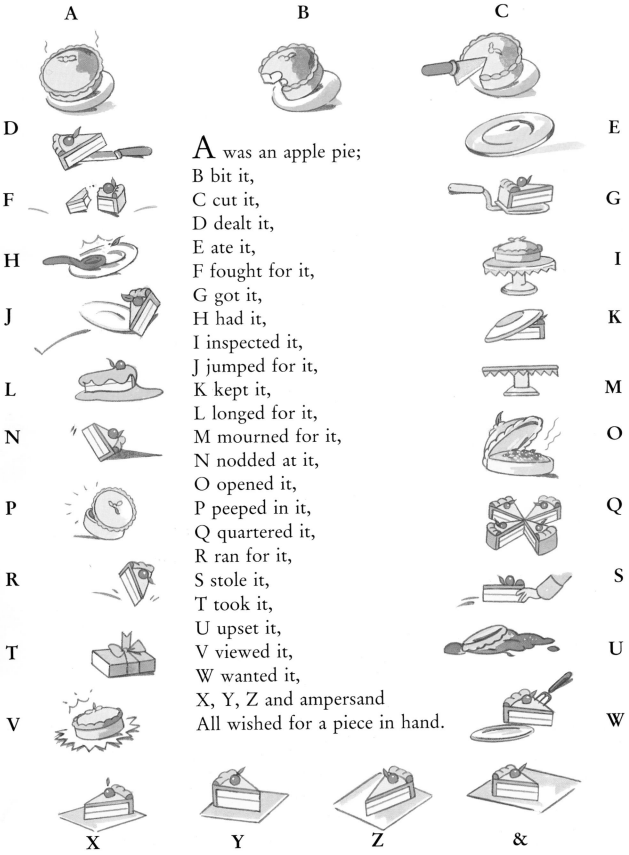

A was an apple pie;
B bit it,
C cut it,
D dealt it,
E ate it,
F fought for it,
G got it,
H had it,
I inspected it,
J jumped for it,
K kept it,
L longed for it,
M mourned for it,
N nodded at it,
O opened it,
P peeped in it,
Q quartered it,
R ran for it,
S stole it,
T took it,
U upset it,
V viewed it,
W wanted it,
X, Y, Z and ampersand
All wished for a piece in hand.

Five little pussycats playing near the door;
  One ran and hid inside
And then there were four.

Four little pussycats underneath a tree;
  One heard a dog bark
And then there were three.

Three little pussycats thinking what to do;
  One saw a little bird
And then there were two.

Two little pussycats sitting in the sun;
  One ran to catch his tail
And then there was one.

One little pussycat looking for some fun;
  He saw a butterfly—
And then there was none.

Here we go round the mulberry bush,
   The mulberry bush, the mulberry bush,
Here we go round the mulberry bush
   So early in the morning.

This is the way we wash our hands,
   Wash our hands, wash our hands,
This is the way we wash our hands
   So early in the morning.

This is the way we wash our face . . .

This is the way we comb our hair . . .

This is the way we tie our shoes . . .

This is the way we go to school . . .

If I were a little bird,
  High in the sky,
I'd flap my wings
  And fly, fly, fly.

If I were a tall giraffe,
  Living in a zoo,
This is how I'd bend my neck
  And look at you.

If I were a friendly dog,
  Going for a run,
This is how I'd wag my tail
  When having fun.

If I were a kangaroo,
  I'd leap and bound.
This is how I'd jump about
  And hop around.

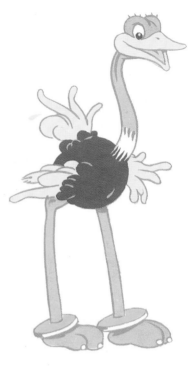

Here is the ostrich straight and tall,
  Nodding his head above us all.

Here is the long snake on the ground,
  Wriggling upon the stones he found.

Here are the birds that fly so high,
  Spreading their wings across the sky.

Here is the hedgehog, prickly, small,
  Rolling himself into a ball.

Here is the spider scuttling around,
  Treading so lightly on the ground.

Here are the children fast asleep,
  And here at night the owls do peep.

Old Macdonald had a farm
 E . . . I . . . E . . . I . . . O
And on that farm he had some cows,
 E . . . I . . . E . . . I . . . O
With a moo-moo here,
 And a moo-moo there,
Here a moo, there a moo,
 Everywhere a moo-moo,
Old Macdonald had a farm
 E . . . I . . . E . . . I . . . O

Old Macdonald had a farm
 E . . . I . . . E . . . I . . . O
And on that farm he had some ducks,
 E . . . I . . . E . . . I . . . O
With a quack-quack here,
 And a quack-quack there,
Here a quack, there a quack,
 Everywhere a quack-quack,
With a moo-moo here,
 And a moo-moo there,
Here a moo, there a moo,
 Everywhere a moo-moo,
Old Macdonald had a farm
 E . . . I . . . E . . . I . . . O

. . . cats . . . meow-meow . . .

. . . horses . . . neigh-neigh . . .

. . . dogs . . . woof-woof . . .

. . . lambs . . . baa-baa . . .

MUSIC SECTION

The music given in this section is for the songs and rhymes
indicated ☆ in the Contents list on page 3.

LULLABIES

The sandman comes

Page 7

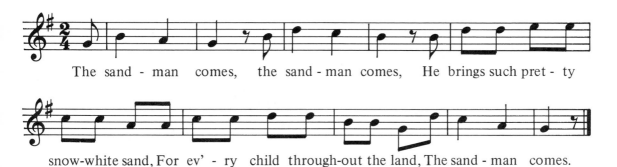

The sand - man comes, the sand - man comes, He brings such pret - ty
snow-white sand, For ev' - ry child through-out the land, The sand - man comes.

Sleep, baby, sleep

Page 8

Sleep, ba - by, sleep, Thy fa - ther guards the
sheep, Thy moth - er shakes the dream - land tree, And
from it fall sweet dreams for thee. Sleep, ba - by, sleep.

Golden slumbers

Page 6

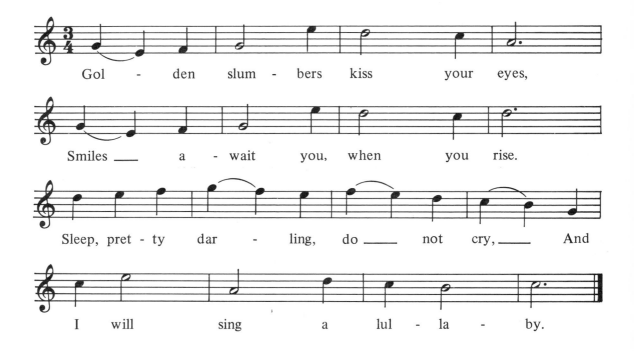

Gol - den slum - bers kiss your eyes,

Smiles __ a - wait you, when you rise.

Sleep, pret - ty dar - ling, do __ not cry, __ And

I will sing a lul - la - by.

Lullaby, and good night

Page 11

Lul - la - by, and good night, In the sky stars are

bright, _ Round your head, __ flo - wers gay __ Scent your slum - bers till

day. Close your eyes now and rest, May these hours __ be

blest, _ Close your eyes now and rest, May these hours __ be blest.

Hush, little baby

Rock-a-bye baby

Page 8

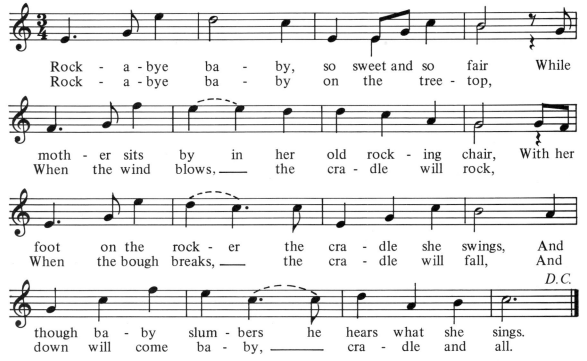

Rock - a - bye ba - by, so sweet and so fair   While
Rock - a - bye ba - by on the tree - top,

moth - er sits by in her old rock - ing chair,   With her
When the wind blows, ___ the cra - dle will rock,

foot on the rock - er the cra - dle she swings,   And
When the bough breaks, ___ the cra - dle will fall,   And

D.C.

though ba - by slum - bers he hears what she sings.
down will come ba - by, ___ cra - dle and all.

Rock-a-bye, rock-a-bye, nothing to fear
Rock-a-bye, rock-a-bye, mother is near;
With her foot on the rocker the cradle she swings,
And though baby slumbers he hears what she sings.

FIRST SONGS

Trot, trot, trot

Page 16

Trot, trot, trot, Go and nev - er stop.

Trudge a - long, my lit - tle po - ny, Where 'tis rough and where 'tis sto - ny.

Go and nev - er stop, Trot, trot, trot, trot, trot!

This is the way the ladies ride

Page 12

This is the way the lad - ies ride: Nim - ble - nim,
This is the way the gen - tle - men ride: Gal - lop - a - trot!
This is the way the far - mers ride: Jig - get - y - jog,
This is the way the butch-er's boy rides: Trip - per - ty - trot,

1.2.3
nim - ble - nim.
Gal - lop - a - trot!
jig - get - y - jog.

4
trip - per - ty trot, Till he falls in a ditch with a

flip - per - ty, Flip - per - ty, flop, flop, FLOP!

Bobby Shaftoe

Page 15

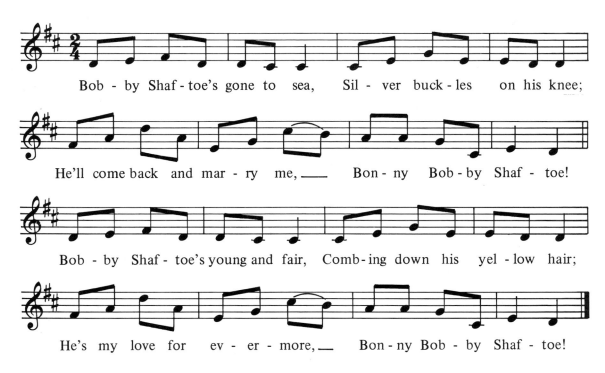

Bob - by Shaf - toe's gone to sea, Sil - ver buck - les on his knee;

He'll come back and mar - ry me, Bon - ny Bob - by Shaf - toe!

Bob - by Shaf - toe's young and fair, Comb - ing down his yel - low hair;

He's my love for ev - er - more, Bon - ny Bob - by Shaf - toe!

To market, to market

Page 16

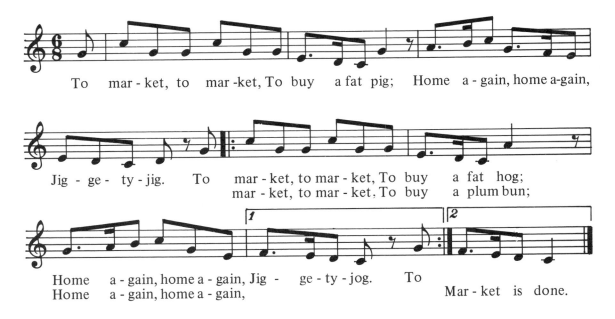

To mar - ket, to mar -ket, To buy a fat pig; Home a - gain, home a-gain,

Jig - ge - ty - jig. To mar - ket, to mar - ket, To buy a fat hog;
mar - ket, to mar - ket, To buy a plum bun;

Home a - gain, home a - gain, Jig - ge - ty - jog. To
Home a - gain, home a - gain,

Mar - ket is done.

This little pig

Page 19

This lit - tle pig went to mar - ket, This lit - tle pig stayed at

home; This lit - tle pig ___ had roast beef,

This lit - tle pig ___ had none. And this lit - tle pig ___ cried:

"Wee - wee - wee - wee - wee," All the way home!

Peek-a-boo

Page 20

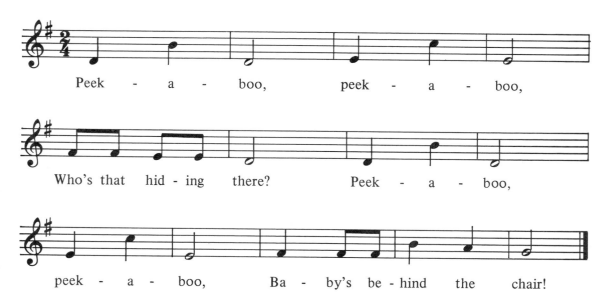

Peek - a - boo, peek - a - boo, Who's that hid - ing there? Peek - a - boo, peek - a - boo, Ba - by's be - hind the chair!

Where, O where

Page 21

Where, O where, has my lit - tle dog gone? O where, O where, can he be? _____ With his tail cut short, and his ears cut long, O where, O where, has he gone? _____

Eensy Weensy Spider

Page 22

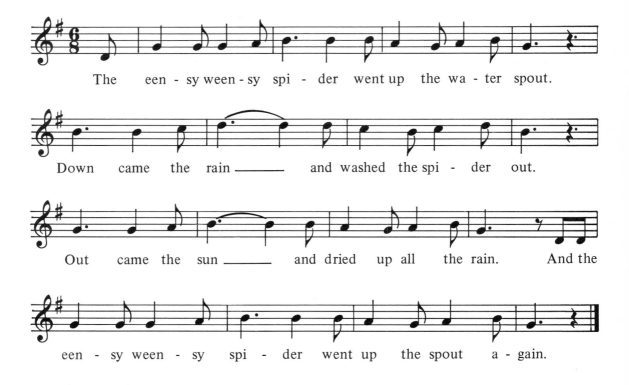

The een - sy ween - sy spi - der went up the wa - ter spout.

Down came the rain ____ and washed the spi - der out.

Out came the sun ____ and dried up all the rain. And the

een - sy ween - sy spi - der went up the spout a - gain.

Little Arabella Miller

Page 23

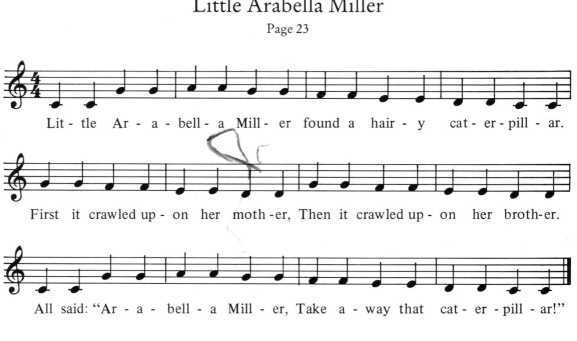

Lit - tle Ar - a - bell - a Mill - er found a hair - y cat - er - pill - ar.

First it crawled up - on her moth - er, Then it crawled up - on her broth - er.

All said: "Ar - a - bell - a Mill - er, Take a - way that cat - er - pill - ar!"

Ride a cockhorse

Page 16

Ride a cock horse to Ban-bur-y Cross, To see a fine la-dy up-on a white horse;

Rings on her fin-gers, And bells on her toes, She shall have mu-sic wher-ev-er she goes.

Hickory, dickory, dock

Page 24

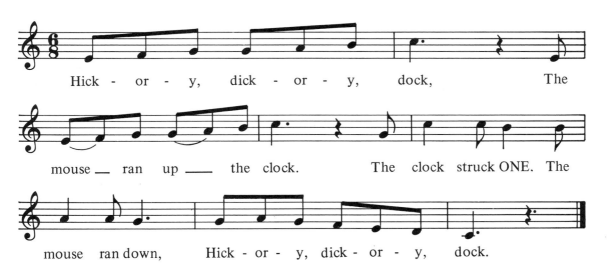

Hick - or - y, dick - or - y, dock, The

mouse ran up the clock. The clock struck ONE. The

mouse ran down, Hick - or - y, dick - or - y, dock.

Row, row, row, your boat

Page 25

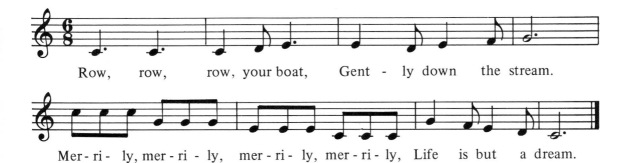

Row, row, row, your boat, Gent - ly down the stream.

Mer - ri - ly, mer - ri - ly, mer - ri - ly, mer - ri - ly, Life is but a dream.

ACTION RHYMES
The farmer's in the dell

Page 40

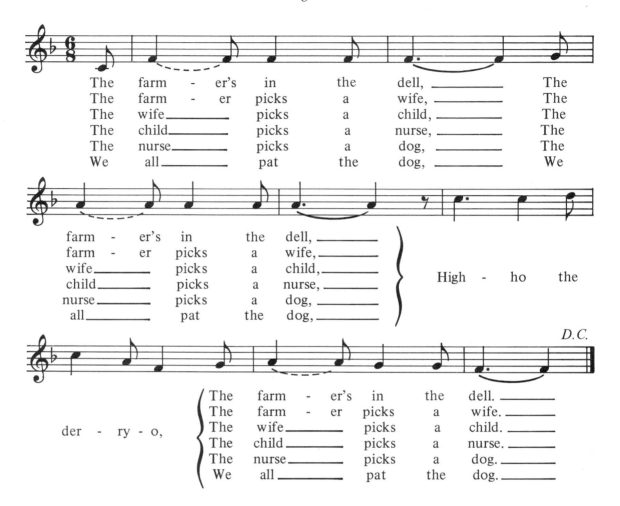

The	farm -	er's	in	the	dell,	_____	The
The	farm -	er	picks	a	wife,	_____	The
The	wife___		picks	a	child,	_____	The
The	child___		picks	a	nurse,	_____	The
The	nurse___		picks	a	dog,	_____	The
We	all___		pat	the	dog,	_____	We

farm -	er's	in	the	dell,	_____
farm -	er	picks	a	wife,	_____
wife___		picks	a	child,	_____
child___		picks	a	nurse,	_____
nurse___		picks	a	dog,	_____
all___		pat	the	dog,	_____

High - ho the

D.C.

der - ry - o,

The	farm -	er's	in	the	dell.	_____
The	farm -	er	picks	a	wife.	_____
The	wife___		picks	a	child.	_____
The	child___		picks	a	nurse.	_____
The	nurse___		picks	a	dog.	_____
We	all___		pat	the	dog.	_____

With my little broom

Page 35

With my lit - tle broom I sweep, sweep, sweep;

On my lit - tle toes I creep, creep, creep.

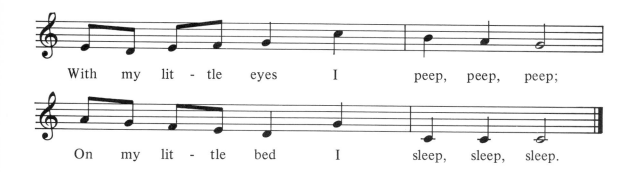

With my lit - tle eyes I peep, peep, peep;

On my lit - tle bed I sleep, sleep, sleep.

I'm a little teapot

Page 28

I'm a lit - tle tea - pot, short and stout. Here is my han - dle, Here is my spout.

When I hear the tea - cups, hear me shout, "Just tip me o - ver, pour me out."

One finger, one thumb

Page 41

One fin - ger, one thumb, ___ keep mov - ing, ___ One

fin - ger, one thumb, ___ keep mov - ing, ___ One fin - ger, one thumb, ___ keep

D.C.

mov - ing, We'll ___ all be mer - ry and bright. ___

The timing of this song will vary as more action phrases are added:

One finger, one thumb, one arm, keep moving . . . . .
One finger, one thumb, one arm, one leg, keep moving . . . . .
One finger, one thumb, one arm, one leg, one nod of the head, keep moving . . .

Down at the station

Page 37

Down at the sta - tion, ear - ly in the morn - ing,

See the lit - tle puf - fer bell - ies all in a row.

See the en - gine dri - ver pull the lit - tle han - dle.

Chug! Chug! Whoo! Whoo! Off we go.

Oh, we can play

Page 36

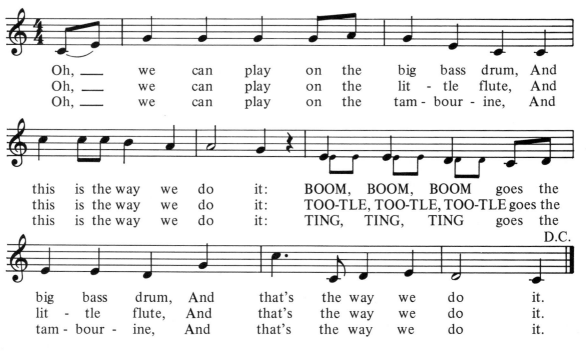

Oh, ___ we can play on the big bass drum, And
Oh, ___ we can play on the lit - tle flute, And
Oh, ___ we can play on the tam - bour - ine, And

this is the way we do it: BOOM, BOOM, BOOM goes the
this is the way we do it: TOO-TLE, TOO-TLE, TOO-TLE goes the
this is the way we do it: TING, TING, TING goes the

D.C.

big bass drum, And that's the way we do it.
lit - tle flute, And that's the way we do it.
tam - bour - ine, And that's the way we do it.

FIDDLE, DIDDLE, DEE goes the violin...   ZOOM, ZOOM, ZOOM goes the double bass...
TICKA, TICKA, TECK go the castanets...   TA, TA, TARA goes the bugle horn...

If you're happy

Page 38

If you're hap - py and you know it,
{ Clap your hands.
{ Nod your head.
{ Say "Ha! Ha!!"
{ Do all three.

If you're hap - py and you know it,
{ Clap your hands.
{ Nod your head.
{ Say "Ha! Ha!!"
{ Do all three.

D.C.

If you're hap - py and you know it, And you real - ly want to show it, If you're hap-py and you know it,
{ Clap your hands.
{ Nod your head.
{ Say "Ha! Ha!!"
{ Do all three.

We are soldiers

Page 29

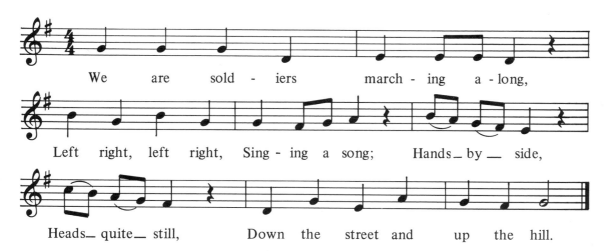

We are sold - iers march - ing a - long,

Left right, left right, Sing - ing a song; Hands by side,

Heads quite still, Down the street and up the hill.

LEARNING RHYMES

One, two, buckle my shoe

Page 42

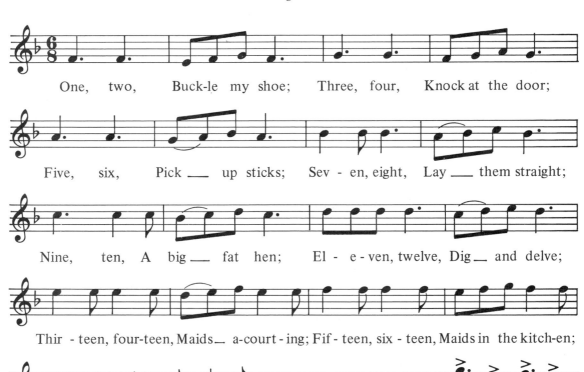

One, two, Buck-le my shoe; Three, four, Knock at the door;

Five, six, Pick __ up sticks; Sev - en, eight, Lay __ them straight;

Nine, ten, A big __ fat hen; El - e - ven, twelve, Dig __ and delve;

Thir - teen, four-teen, Maids __ a-court-ing; Fif - teen, six - teen, Maids in the kitch-en;

Sev - en - teen, eight - een, Maids in wait - ing; Nine-teen, twen-ty, My plate's emp-ty.

If I were a little bird

Page 46

If I were a lit - tle bird, High ____ in the sky,
If I were a tall gir - affe, Liv - ing in a zoo,
If I were a friend - ly dog, Go - ing for a run,
If I were a kang - a - roo, I'd ____ leap and bound.

I'd flap my wings And ____ fly, fly, fly.
This is how I'd bend my neck And look at you.
This is how I'd wag my tail When hav - ing fun.
This is how I'd jump a - bout And hop a - round.

Here we go round the mulberry bush
Page 45

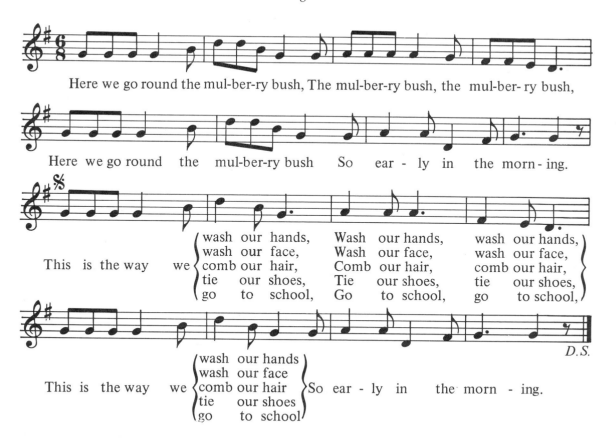

Here we go round the mul-ber-ry bush, The mul-ber-ry bush, the mul-ber-ry bush,

Here we go round the mul-ber-ry bush So ear-ly in the morn-ing.

This is the way we
{ wash our hands, Wash our hands, wash our hands,
wash our face, Wash our face, wash our face,
comb our hair, Comb our hair, comb our hair,
tie our shoes, Tie our shoes, tie our shoes,
go to school, Go to school, go to school, }

This is the way we
{ wash our hands
wash our face
comb our hair
tie our shoes
go to school }
So ear-ly in the morn-ing.

D.S.

Five little pussycats
Page 44

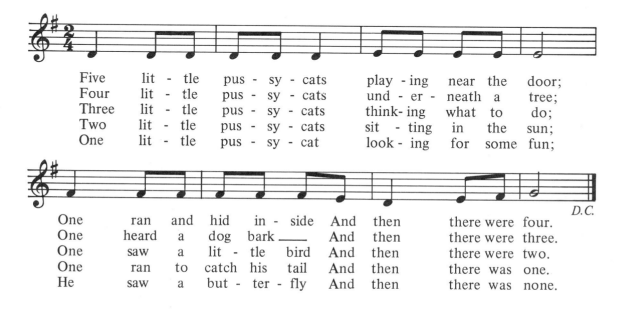

Five lit - tle pus - sy - cats play - ing near the door;
Four lit - tle pus - sy - cats und - er - neath a tree;
Three lit - tle pus - sy - cats think- ing what to do;
Two lit - tle pus - sy - cats sit - ting in the sun;
One lit - tle pus - sy - cat look- ing for some fun;

One ran and hid in - side And then there were four.
One heard a dog bark ___ And then there were three.
One saw a lit - tle bird And then there were two.
One ran to catch his tail And then there was one.
He saw a but - ter - fly And then there was none.

D.C.

Old Macdonald

Page 48

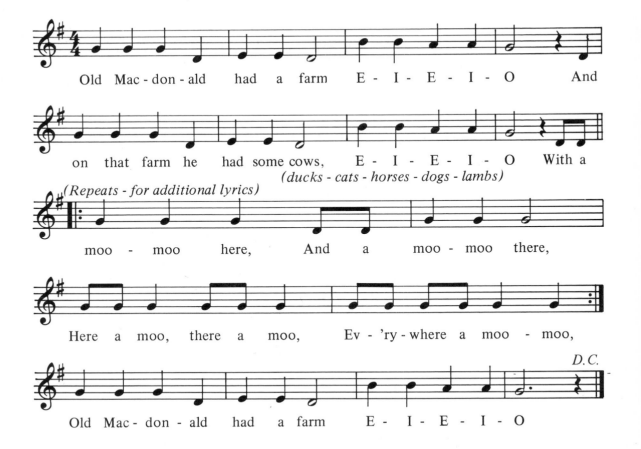

Old Mac - don - ald had a farm E - I - E - I - O And

on that farm he had some cows, E - I - E - I - O With a
(ducks - cats - horses - dogs - lambs)

(Repeats - for additional lyrics)

moo - moo here, And a moo - moo there,

Here a moo, there a moo, Ev - 'ry - where a moo - moo,

D.C.

Old Mac - don - ald had a farm E - I - E - I - O

Old Macdonald had a farm
E - I - E - I - O
And on that farm he had some ducks,
E - I - E - I - O
With a quack-quack here,
And a quack-quack there,
Here a quack, there a quack,
Everywhere a quack-quack,
With a moo-moo here,
And a moo-moo- there,
Here a moo, there a moo,
Everywhere a moo-moo,
Old Macdonald had a farm
E - I - E - I - O

...cats.......meow-meow...
...horses...neigh-neigh...
...dogs......woof-woof...
...lambs....baa-baa...